TAXI

WALTER
DOES HIS BEST

WALTER
DOES HIS BEST

A FRENCHIE ADVENTURE
IN KINDNESS AND MUDDY PAWS

EVA PILGRIM

ILLUSTRATED BY
Jessica Gibson

An Imprint of Thomas Nelson

To Ed, who always cleans up Walter's messes.

—E.P.

To Walter. Good job, Walter!

—J.G.

Hey there! I'm Walter. I live with my mom in New York City. I sleep. I eat. I really, really like treats. But . . . exercise?

Fer-Snerrrt!

I hate walks. I know people think dogs like to walk. Well, I don't.

"WALTER!"

PLOP!

"Please. Try to be good. We've got a lot to do today. A good dog is kind and helpful and obedient."

Oh my biscuits!
There's a good, kind,
and helpful dog.

And she gets to ride in a car.
No walking.

I bet that car has treats.
I bet that dog can see
everything from in there!

I want to ride in a car.

I

CAN BE A

GOOD DOG

TOO!

Good dogs help their neighbors.

Jorge's flower beds always need work, and I'm a good digger!

I can fertilize. And I can water.

I'm a good dog. Look at me!

Good dogs are kind to strangers.
I like my comfy spot,
but that guy needs a seat.

oww-roo.

Here you go, sir!

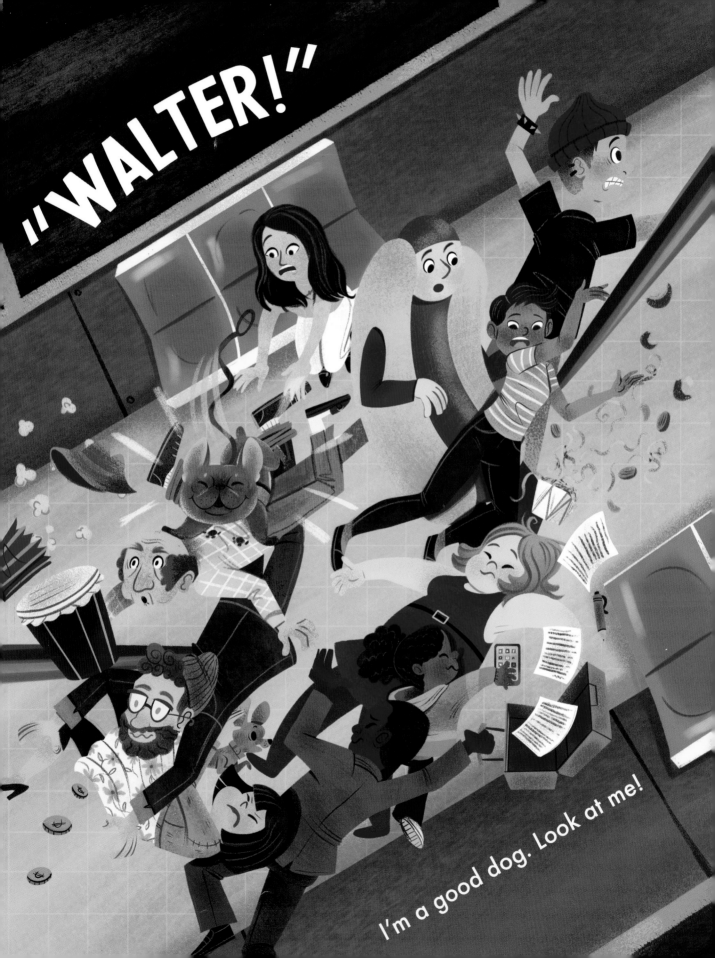

Good dogs are thoughtful.

My friend Gabby is sad.
I can fix that!

I'm a good dog. Look at me!

I've been such a good dog.
I'm basically a super dog.
It's time for a ride!

Fine. I can be even better.
Good dogs pitch in when
others are in trouble.

WATCH OUT!

STOP!

"WALTER!"

I'm a good dog. Look at me!

Good dogs make people smile. My mom loves when I show off my tricks.

SIT.

STAND.

Spin.

whoo-hoo!

SPLASH!
SPLITTER SPLATTER
SMASH!

"WALTER!"

I'm a good dog. Look at me!

Good dogs encourage others.
This poor actor.
The crowd is giving him nothing.

I will give him everything I've got!

"WALTER.
SHHHH!"

"You two.
Out of here!"

Fer-Snerrrt!

I was a good dog all day,
and no one even noticed.
I encouraged.
I helped.
I pitched in when there was a need.
I was thoughtful.
I was kind.

And now, I'm

TIRED.

This is what I get after a long day of trying to be good?

A bath?!

I hate baths.
I hate having my nails clipped.
And keep that thing out of my ears.

Grrrrr!

"Walter, come along.
I have a surprise for you."

"Walter, you don't have to be perfect to be kind. You don't even have to get it right all of the time."

"And even though you think no one notices . . . people do."

"WALTER, I'M SO GLAD I HAVE YOU!"

Oh my biscuits!

Look at me.

I'M A GOOD DOG!

Walter Does His Best: A Frenchie Adventure in Kindness and Muddy Paws

© 2021 Eva Pilgrim

Tommy Nelson, PO Box 141000, Nashville, TN 37214

Published in Nashville, Tennessee, by Tommy Nelson. Tommy Nelson is an imprint of Thomas Nelson. Thomas Nelson is a registered trademark of HarperCollins Christian Publishing, Inc.

Tommy Nelson titles may be purchased in bulk for educational, business, fundraising, or sales promotional use. For information, please e-mail SpecialMarkets@ThomasNelson.com.

Illustrated by Jessica Gibson

Library of Congress Cataloging-in-Publication Data

Names: Pilgrim, Eva, 1982- author. | Gibson, Jessica (Illustrator), illustrator.
Title: Walter does his best : a Frenchie adventure in kindness and muddy paws / by Eva Pilgrim ; illustrations by Jessica Gibson.
Description: Nashville, TN : Tommy Nelson, [2021] | Audience: Ages 4-8. | Summary: Accompanying his busy human around New York City, Walter tries to be a good dog.
Identifiers: LCCN 2021003908 (print) | LCCN 2021003909 (ebook) | ISBN 9781400226771 (hardcover) | ISBN 9781400226788 (epub)
Subjects: CYAC: French bulldog--Fiction. | Bulldog--Fiction. | Dogs--Fiction. | Kindness--Fiction. | Humorous stories. | New York(N.Y.)--Fiction.
Classification: LCC PZ7.1.P5533 Wal 2021 (print) | LCC PZ7.1.P5533 (ebook) | DDC [E]--dc23
LC record available at https://lccn.loc.gov/2021003908
LC ebook record available at https://lccn.loc.gov/2021003909

Printed in Korea

21 22 23 24 25 SAM 10 9 8 7 6 5 4 3 2 1

Mfr: SAM / Seoul, Korea / September 2021 / PO #12040400